Rock It!™

MAR 2011

FOSSILS
HISTORY IN THE ROCKS

Steven M. Hoffman

PowerKiDS press.

New York

Published in 2011 by The Rosen Publishing Group, Inc.
29 East 21st Street, New York, NY 10010

First Edition

Editor: Amelie von Zumbusch
Book Design: Kate Laczynski
Layout Design: Ashley Burrell

Photo Credits: Cover iStockphoto/Thinkstock; pp. 4, 18 Ken Lucas/Getty Images; pp. 6, 8, 10, 16 (inset) Shutterstock.com; p. 12 Colin Keates/Getty Images; p. 14 G. R. "Dick" Roberts/ NSIL/Getty Images; p. 16 (main) Michael Melford/Getty Images; p. 20 David McNew/Getty Images.

Library of Congress Cataloging-in-Publication Data

Hoffman, Steven M. (Steven Michael), 1960-
 Fossils : history in the rocks / by Steven M. Hoffman. — 1st ed.
      p. cm. — (Rock it!)
 Includes index.
 ISBN 978-1-4488-2558-5 (library binding) — ISBN 978-1-4488-2702-2 (pbk.) —
ISBN 978-1-4488-2703-9 (6-pack)
 1. Fossils—Juvenile literature. 2. Paleontology—Juvenile literature. I. Title.
 QE714.5.H58 2011
 560—dc22
                                        2010030247

Manufactured in the United States of America

CPSIA Compliance Information: Batch #WW11PK: For Further Information contact Rosen Publishing, New York, New York at 1-800-237-9932

CONTENTS

This turtle fossil was found in Wyoming. It is part of a group of fossils called the Green River formation. These fossils show that the area was once hotter and wetter than it is today.

Clues to Past Life

How do we know that some dinosaurs had spikes on their tails? Dinosaurs lived long ago. People were not alive to see them. We know what they looked like by studying their fossils. Fossils are any remains or traces of something that lived in the distant past. Fossils are found in rocks. They hold clues about Earth's past.

Most fossils form when parts of living things are buried by sand or mud. These parts are sometimes bones. They could also be teeth, eggs, shells, or pieces of wood. After an object is buried, the sand or mud slowly changes to rock. The object becomes a fossil.

Many of these fossilized shells are cast fossils. Molds and casts are the most commonly found kinds of fossils.

Molds and Casts

There are many kinds of fossils. Mold fossils are holes that have the shapes of living things. Shells are common mold fossils. A mold fossil often forms when water soaks into the rock where a shell is buried. The water **dissolves** the shell. The matter that makes up the shell is swept away in the water. This leaves a mold, or shell-shaped hole. You can see the shell's markings on the inside of the mold.

Sometimes, a mold fills with mud or sand. The mud or sand hardens into a piece of rock that has the shape of the thing from which the mold formed. It becomes a kind of fossil called a cast.

The trees in Arizona's petrified forest are about 225 million years old. The colorful fossils are made mostly of the mineral quartz.

Bone to Stone

Some objects, such as bone and wood, have holes in them that are too tiny to see. When these objects get buried, water may seep into these holes. This water often has **minerals**, such as quartz, in it. The minerals come out of the water and fill the holes. This is known as **permineralization**. The trees of Arizona's petrified forest became fossils this way.

Bone, wood, and shell can also become replacement fossils. This happens when minerals that come out of water take the place of the bits of matter that make up an object.

Some fossil shells have a pretty gold color because they were changed to the mineral pyrite, or fool's gold.

This piece of amber has a small, fossilized frog in it!
Amber is also sometimes known as fossil resin.

Soft Parts and Tracks

Soft parts of animals, such as skin and meat, usually rot. They do not often become fossils. However, the soft-part fossils that do occur tell people more about the animal than bones or shells could. Fossils of hairy, elephant-like animals, called mammoths, have been found in frozen ground. The hair and meat is still in good condition. Whole **insect** fossils have been found in amber, or hardened tree sap.

Trace fossils are another kind of fossil. They are fossil tracks, **burrows**, or other marks that animals made in sand or mud. Fossilized dinosaur footprints and eggs are both trace fossils.

Plant leaves often end up as compression fossils. When heavy rocks form above a buried leaf, the matter of the leaf is flattened. It becomes a compression fossil.

This fossil of an animal called a crustacean was found in limestone. Limestone is one of the rocks in which people most often find fossils.

Closed in Stone

Fossils usually occur in **sedimentary rock**. This kind of rock forms when bits of matter, called sediment, are pressed together. Sedimentary rocks that hold fossils are usually made from mud or sand. These rocks often form along rivers and at the bottoms of oceans and lakes. The remains of living things get caught in the mud or sand that builds up in these places. When this sediment changes to rock, the remains become fossils.

Some sedimentary rock is made almost completely of fossils. The sedimentary rock limestone is made of animal shells or the remains of tiny plantlike **algae**.

Corals are tiny animals that form communities called reefs. The outside of a reef has living coral, while the inside is made of dead coral. Fossil coral reefs are known as reef rock.

You can see many layers in this rock face along the side of a road on New Zealand's North Island.

Bottom to Top

Sedimentary rocks usually form in **layers**. When layers of mud and sand build up, the top layers push down heavily on the bottom ones. This **pressure** helps turn the bottom layers into rock.

You know that the bottom pancake in a stack was put down first. Just like in a stack of pancakes, the oldest layer of sedimentary rock is on the bottom. The layers get younger from bottom to top. As you might guess, the oldest fossils are found in the lowest layers of rock. Younger fossils are found closer to the top. Fossils in the same layer are from animals and plants that lived at about the same time.

This trilobite proves that the rocks in which it was found formed around 500 million years ago. Inset: This trilobite dates the rocks around it to between 415 and 360 million years ago.

Fossils of All Kinds

Many kinds of fossils are found only in rock layers of a certain age. Some fossils are common in a particular rock layer. People can recognize when a rock formed by spotting these fossils. Trilobite fossils are used for this purpose. Trilobites were animals that lived in the ocean. They had three **lobes** and were small.

Less common fossils, such as nests full of dinosaur eggs, can also teach us a lot. **Tar pits** are a good source for uncommon fossils. The bones and long teeth of animals called saber-toothed tigers have been found there.

Shark teeth are common fossils in some places. They can be as small as your teeth or as large as your hand.

This fossil is of the dinosaur Coelophysis bauri. *It is one of several* Coelophysis bauri *fossils that were found in New Mexico.*

The Story of Life

The fossils in Earth's rocks show us how life on Earth has changed over time. We can see what kinds of fossils formed at different times in the past. Together, all of Earth's fossils are known as the fossil record.

One of the things we have learned from the fossil record is that dinosaurs roamed Earth for almost 200 million years. Then they disappeared about 65 million years ago. Scientists wondered what caused this. They now know from looking at rocks that a **meteorite** hit Earth. The meteorite sent rock dust into the air, blocking out the Sun. Plants died and animals, such as dinosaurs, could not find food to eat.

This scientist is studying fossils from a tar pit in what is now Los Angeles, California. The fossils are between 10,000 and 40,000 years old.

The Fossil Hunt

Many people hunt for fossils. It is hard work, but it is also fun. Fossil hunters begin by looking at rocks that are likely to have fossils. When they find a rock with a fossil, they take notes. They describe the fossil and the rocks around it.

Fossil hunters then use **trowels**, brushes, and other tools to free and clean the fossil. Fossil bones are often wrapped in plaster casts. These keep the bones from breaking when they are moved.

Finally, the fossil may be taken to a **museum** or school. There, scientists study fossils to learn about the living things that made the fossils.

Starting a Collection

A good way to learn about fossils is by beginning a collection. Fossils occur in many places, some near your home. Look at pieces of rock that you pass. The stones in a driveway can hold many fossils. The rocks in a field or park also might have fossils. Teachers may know places where fossils can be found.

As you build your collection, study each fossil you find. Try to imagine how the plant or animal looked and how it lived. Remember that each fossil tells a story of past life. With a little practice, you can learn to read this story as easily as you read a book.

GLOSSARY

algae (AL-jee) Plantlike living things without roots or stems that live in water.

burrows (BUR-ohz) Holes animals dig in the ground for shelter.

dissolves (dih-ZOLVZ) Breaks down or fades away.

insect (IN-sekt) A small creature that often has six legs and wings.

layers (LAY-erz) Thicknesses of something.

lobes (LOHBZ) Rounded parts that stick out or down.

meteorite (MEE-tee-uh-ryt) A rock from outer space that reaches Earth's surface.

minerals (MIN-rulz) Natural things that are not animals, plants, or other living things.

museum (myoo-ZEE-um) A place where a collection of art or historical pieces are safely kept for people to see and to study.

permineralization (pir-min-ruh-luh-ZAY-shun) The building up of minerals that leads to fossil formation.

pressure (PREH-shur) A force that pushes on something.

sedimentary rock (seh-deh-MEN-teh-ree ROK) Layers of stones, sand, or mud that have been pressed together to form rock.

tar pits (TAHR PITS) Places where matter called bitumen has leaked aboveground to form thick, sticky pools.

trowels (TROW-elz) Small shovels.

INDEX

B
bone(s), 5, 9, 11,
17, 21

D
dinosaurs, 5, 19

E
eggs, 5, 11, 17

L
layer(s), 15, 17

M
meteorite, 19

minerals, 9
mud, 5, 7, 11, 13, 15
museum, 21

P
permineralization, 9
pressure, 15

R
remains, 5, 13

S
sand, 5, 7, 11, 13, 15
sedimentary rock, 13,
15

shell(s), 5, 7, 9, 11,
13
spikes, 5

T
tails, 5
tar pits, 17
teeth, 5, 17
traces, 5
trowels, 21

W
water, 7, 9
wood, 5, 9

WEB SITES

Due to the changing nature of Internet links, PowerKids Press has developed an online list of Web sites related to the subject of this book. This site is updated regularly. Please use this link to access the list: www.powerkidslinks.com/rockit/fossils/